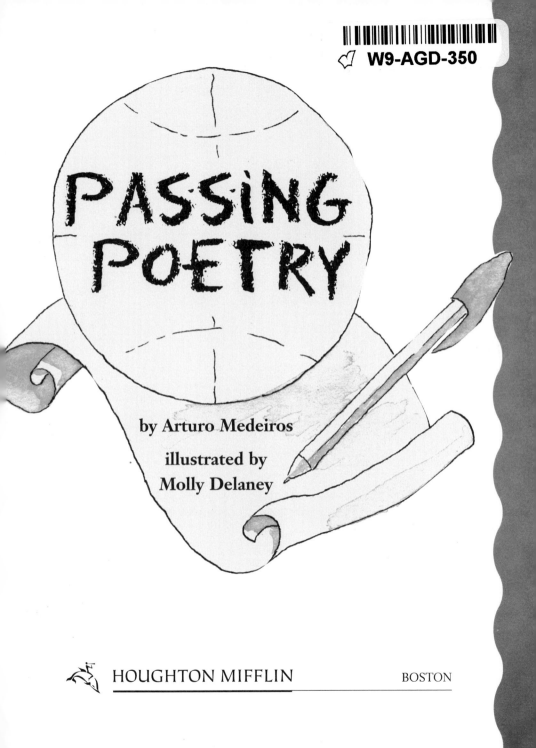

PASSING POETRY

by Arturo Medeiros

illustrated by
Molly Delaney

HOUGHTON MIFFLIN   BOSTON

Alison caught the ball from Karim and took a shot. The ball banked on the metal backboard and into the basket. Game. The two of them slapped hands, and then walked off the court with their friends Jordan and Elisa.

"Good game," Alison said.

Jordan nodded. "For you, especially," he said. "I don't think you missed a shot . . . oh, except that one that I blocked. Just jumped up and—" He swatted an imaginary ball away.

Alison rolled her eyes. "Oh, do you think you could have blocked that one if I hadn't let you?" she asked. "I just wasn't trying, because I didn't want you crying."

"Hey, say that again," Karim said. "I think I'm hearing things. Are you a poet?"

Alison thought for a moment. Then she repeated her words.

"I just wasn't trying,
Because I didn't want you crying."

"Hey, you're right, Karim," Alison said. "Maybe our poetry class is getting to me."

"You must have been paying attention to Mr. Hill," Jordan added.

Karim laughed. "Hey, you've got to pay attention to Mr. Hill. Unless you enjoy detention."

"Most of the time, I do pay attention," Jordan answered. "I just have a hard time following all the poetry stuff we've been doing."

"Well, you better catch on quickly," Elisa said. "Our poems are due next week."

The next morning before class, Alison handed Karim a note. He opened it and read,

I dribble and look you in the eye
You reach for the ball as I run by,
but miss the ball you tried to get
I shoot and bank it in the net.
                    —Alison

Karim looked up at her. "What's this about?" he asked.

"Practice for poetry class," she said. "Write down your own, and then pass it on to Elisa."

"I understand that part," he answered, "but what makes you think you can get by me?"

Alison smiled. "Because I do every time we play. So go write your poem."

Karim sat and thought. No poem came to mind. The bell rang, and Mr. Hill started class. It was math, first subject of the day. Karim paid attention at first, but then remembered the poem. His mind wandered.

Finally, something clicked, and he began scribbling in the margin of his notebook. He had written two lines when a voice boomed from the front of the classroom.

"Karim."

He looked up, and saw Mr. Hill looking at him, expecting an answer. "Yes sir?"

"The remainder for this equation?" Mr. Hill said slowly.

Karim looked at the board and did a quick mental calculation. "Seven," he answered.

Mr. Hill nodded. "Very good." He continued with the lesson. Karim sighed with relief, and went back to his poem. Soon, he had a limerick:

Elisa—
You want a teammate who passes
So will you allow me to ask this:
Please team up with me
And then you will see
What it feels like to score your own baskets.
                    — Karim

He waited until lunchtime, and then quickly added his note to Alison's. In the cafeteria, he handed it to Elisa.

She read it and laughed. "Okay, it's a deal. You and I team up today." She paused. "Now I've got to write a good one for Jordan."

Halfway through English class, Jordan got a note from Elisa. At the bottom was her poem:

A bright orange ball
Drops. —You bounce it off your foot.
No basket for you.

Jordan reread the note, and then looked at Elisa. "You didn't write a poem," he whispered.

"Yes I did," she answered. "It's a haiku."

"No. It doesn't rhyme," Jordan whispered back.

"It doesn't matter," Elisa hissed under her breath. "Haiku is a kind of Japanese poem. It doesn't have to rhyme."

A shadow loomed behind them, and a hand reached over Jordan's shoulder and plucked the note. Mr. Hill stood above them, reading.

"Alison, Karim, Elisa, Jordan. After class."

The rest of the day crept along. Finally, the bell rang, and the four students gathered in front of Mr. Hill's desk.

Mr. Hill looked at them sternly, and then spoke. "You young poets know you are not to pass notes in my class. But," he continued, "I'm glad you're taking poetry so seriously." He paused, and gave a hint of a smile. "If you write any more poetry in my class, I want to see it first!"

Surprised, they thanked him, and turned to leave. As they reached the doorway, Alison spoke up.

"Mr. Hill, can we use the poems we wrote for our assignment?"

Raising an eyebrow, Mr. Hill said:

"No."

"Go."

They walked out of the classroom, heading towards the basketball court.

"That," said Jordan, "has got to be the shortest poem I've ever heard."